P9-BZR-085

NANNY NOONY and the MAGIC SPELL

by Edward Frascino

PIPPIN PRESS
New York

Published by Pippin Press, New York

Printed in Spain .J

10 9 8 7 6 5 4 3 2 1

Library of Congress Cataloging-in-Publication Data
Frascino, Edward
Nanny Noony and the Magic Spell
Summary: When a magic spell is cast on a farm causing everyone to act contrary, the cat decides to find out who did it.
[1. Farm life—Fiction. 2. Cats—Fiction. 3. Witches—Fiction. 4. Magic—Fiction] I. Title.
PZ7.F8596Nan 1988 [E] 88-12420
ISBN 0-945912-00-5

"Where is the milk?" asked the farmer's wife.

"The cow won't give a drop," said the farmer.

"Where are the eggs?" asked the farmer's wife.

"The hens have stopped laying," said the farmer. "I'll have to go to market to buy our breakfast."

He climbed on his mule, but the animal kicked and brayed, knocking the farmer to the ground.

"That sheep is going bald," said the farmer's wife, picking up clumps of wool scattered over the barnyard. "And something's

ailing that pig. He just lies on his back staring up at the sky."

The farmer and his wife each blamed the other for their misfortunes, and soon they were quarreling noisily.

The cat, who had been out all night, came home to the sound of angry voices.

"Good morning," said the cat to the chickens, who flapped their wings and pecked him.

"Lovely morning," the cat greeted the sheep.

"My wool! My wool!" bleated the sheep, zigzagging in circles. "Baaaaaa!"

"I don't believe it," thought the cat, as he looked up and saw the cow eating the roof of the farmhouse.

"How did she get up there?" the cat said to the pig, but the pig didn't bat an eye.

"What's wrong with everyone?" the cat asked his friend the mule, and to his great surprise the mule kicked him.

"That settles it," said the cat. "I'm going visiting until everyone around here gets normal again."

The first farm he came to looked cozy and friendly until a big dog came running out of the farmhouse and almost caught the cat's tail.

There was no dog at the next farm but the fat calico cat who lived there arched her back and hissed, "This farm isn't big enough for the both of us."

"Haw! Haw! Haw! You're smart not to mess with that calico."

Looking up, the cat saw a big, red-eyed blackbird sitting in a tree.

"You look troubled, friend," said the blackbird. "Maybe I can help."

"I haven't heard a kind word all day," said the cat, and he told the blackbird of the trouble on his farm. "It's a mystery."

"It may seem like a mystery to you, but up there in the sky I can see more than you folks on the ground."

"Do you mean you know why everyone is acting so strangely?"

"I do," said the blackbird. "Nanny Noony has put a hex on your farm."

"Who is Nanny Noony?" asked the cat.

"She's a witch," said the blackbird.

"Why would she hex our farm?"

"Because she is wicked. Witches don't need any more reason than that," said the blackbird. "But you could undo the hex if you had her 'Book Of Potions.' All her secrets are written down in it."

"Where is this witch?" asked the cat.

"In there." The blackbird pointed a feather toward the thick, dark woods.

"Thank you," said the cat, and he walked bravely into the woods.

"So long, friend," said the blackbird, and he flew away.

In the thickest, darkest part of the woods the cat came upon a huge tree with a door and a window and a smoking chimney in it.

"I've climbed many a tree but I've never seen one like that before," the cat said to himself, and he climbed up and looked in the window.

Inside he saw a tiny, old woman stirring a big, black cauldron. She sang:

Nanny Noony
is my name.
Brewing potions
is my game.

On top of her head, tied tightly in place with a red bandana, was a book.

That must be the "Book of Potions," thought the cat.

"Come in," said Nanny Noony without turning around. "I know you're there."

Does this witch have eyes in the back of her head?, wondered the cat. He didn't know that she saw his reflection in the bright, copper tea kettle on the floor.

If only I can knock that book off her head, thought the cat, climbing through the window.

He arched his back and with all his strength, bumped the stool Nanny Noony stood on. The old woman toppled to the floor.

"What are you trying to do," cried Nanny Noony, "break my back?"

The book stayed firmly on her head.

As Nanny Noony stood up, the cat ran between her feet, knocking her right out of her wooden shoes, but the "Book of Potions" did not budge.

"What ails you, Cat?"

"You wicked old witch," the cat hissed. "You hexed my farm."

"Where'd you hear that nonsense?" asked Nanny Noony.

"A red-eyed blackbird," began the cat.

"Say no more," interrupted Nanny Noony. "Ol' Evil Eye is up to his tricks again. That bird hexed your farm."

He says she did and she says he did, thought the cat. *I don't know who to believe.*

"Haw! Haw! Haw!" Suddenly the blackbird flew into the tree trunk.

"Shoo! Evil Eye!" Nanny Noony swung her broom in the air. "I'll have none of your mischief around here."

“Did you see that, friend?” the blackbird cried. “She tried to kill me.”

“Begone!” said Nanny Noony, “before someone bakes you into a pie.”

“OOOOOOOOOW!” the blackbird moaned. “She’s putting a hex on me.”

He fluttered about in the air, twitched once, and fell to the floor in a heap of black feathers.

"He's faking," said Nanny Noony. "He hopes to catch me off guard so that he can steal my 'Book of Potions.' It contains the remedies for all his evil spells."

The cat stared at the blackbird lying stone still.

I don't believe her, he decided.

"MEOOOW!" the cat began to sob. "First my farm, then my friend. Now, I fear, this witch is going to hex me."

His whiskers grew quite soggy with tears.

"Poor thing," said Nanny Noony. "Here, dry your eyes." And she untied her red bandana and gave it to the cat.

Instantly the blackbird streaked through the air and plucked the "Book of Potions" off Nanny Noony's head.

"You *were* faking," said the cat.

"Haw! Haw! Haw!" cackled the blackbird. "Now the book is mine and no one can undo my hexes."

"I warned you not to trust that villain," said Nanny Noony.

"Nice work, friend." the blackbird said to the cat. "You deserve a reward. How about a little game of cat and mouse?"

Point a feather
at this kitty.
See him shrink
and have no pity.

The cat grew smaller and smaller until he was looking at himself in the side of the bright, copper tea kettle. He was no bigger than a nutshell.

"Here, Mousey, Mousey!" called the blackbird, and a big, fat mouse scurried in through a hole in the tree trunk.

"You look hungry, Mr. Mouse," said the blackbird. "How about a nice juicy kitty-cat for dinner?"

The mouse, who was a giant to the shrunken cat, began chasing him around the floor.

"Not so fast," said Nanny Noony, and reaching into her apron pocket, she tossed a chunk of cheese in front of the mouse, who stopped in his tracks and began nibbling at it.

"You meddlesome old crone," said the blackbird.

Point a feather
at my foe.
Make her eyebrows
white with snow.

A frosty gust of wind blew through the tree trunk, leaving Nanny Noony frozen solid.

"Enough of this sport," said the blackbird, pointing at the cat. "I'm afraid I must bid you farewell, friend."

The cat looked desperately for a place to hide.

Point a feather
at my foe.
See him vanish
head to toe.

Just as the blackbird uttered the last words of the hex, the cat jumped into the tea kettle.

"GADZOOKS!" shrieked the blackbird pointing at his own reflection in the side of the kettle. "I've hexed myself!" And he vanished into thin air, from head to toe.

At the same moment the ice around Nanny Noony melted, and the cat popped back to his normal size.

Meanwhile, back at the farm, the cow gave milk, the hens laid eggs, the sheep's wool grew thick, and the mule stopped kicking.

"What happened?" asked the pig, standing up and shaking himself.

The farmer and his wife kissed and made up.

Nanny Noony brewed a special potion for the farmer, and he had the biggest, juiciest harvest in the land.